The Honey Jar
·
Rigoberta Menchú

WITH Dante Liano

PICTURES BY

Domi

TRANSLATED BY David Unger

GROUNDWOOD BOOKS
HOUSE OF ANANSI PRESS
TORONTO   BERKELEY

A Cirenia y Paulino, mis padres
– Domi

Groundwood Books / House of Anansi Press
110 Spadina Avenue, Suite 801, Toronto M5V 2K4

Distributed in the USA by Publishers Group West
1700 Fourth Street, Berkeley, CA 94710

Library and Archives Canada Cataloguing in Publication
The honey jar / Rigoberta Menchú with Dante Liano; pictures by Domi;
translated by David Unger.
Translation of: El vaso de miel.
ISBN-13: 978-0-88899-670-1.–ISBN-10: 0-88899-670-5
1. Mayas–Folklore. 2. Tales–Guatemala. 3. Maya mythology–Juvenile literature. I. Liano, Dante
II. Unger, David III. Domi IV. Title.
PZ7.M53Ho 2006   j398.2'089'974207281   C2005-905279-1

The illustrations are in oils.
Printed and bound in China

Table of Contents

The Honey Jar

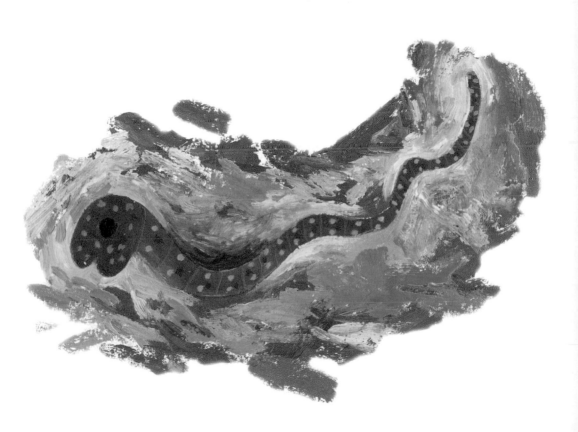

Grandmother Moon and Grandfather Sun Were Bored

W<small>HEN</small> I <small>WAS</small> a little girl in Chimel, my birthplace, the village festival was a special holiday. Actually, we celebrated many holidays throughout the year – for New Year's, Holy Week, planting and harvesting, marriages and the Day of the Dead.

The children would always ask, "How much longer till the planting festival?" or "How much longer till the Holy Week processions?" and "When will we receive the gifts of the harvest holiday?" We kids had no patience. We went around asking our parents all sorts of questions, tugging on their skirts or coat sleeves. We were always waiting for something. And when one festival ended, we were ready for the next.

But the holiday we looked forward to most of all was the village festival. There were always lots of sweets and food and a procession, followed by dancing all day long. We kids would scamper among the dancers who wore masks representing the sun, the moon and the stars. They danced in circles because the heavenly bodies move in circles.

Chattering all the while, the women would walk from one end of the village to the other. They resembled a flower garden as they showed off their multicolored *huipiles*. Our parents would explain why the elders put on their fanciest costumes, and why the dancers – especially the sun and the moon – danced the whole day long. They were creating the world anew, playing out the story of thousands of years ago when Grandfather Sun reflected himself in the face of Grandmother Moon and saw a trace of sadness.

Actually, Grandmother Moon was very, very sad. And when Grandfather Sun saw this, he realized that he had been feeling the same sadness for many hundreds of years.

Grandmother Moon and Grandfather Sun lived suspended in the sky with the cotton-candy clouds. Whenever they wanted, they'd grab a cotton ball, which was really a shred of cloud, and they'd eat this pink, orange and blue cotton. And it was oh, so sweet, because the cotton-candy clouds were made by spinning either white or brown sugar, depending on the season.

Although Grandfather Sun was in love with Grandmother Moon and could see his own light reflected in his wife's face, he knew something was missing. And so in the darkness that only Grandfather Sun with his golden hair and Grandmother Moon with her white eyelids could illuminate, they created stars from the four hundred boys that appeared in the sacred book, the Popul Vuh. And Grandmother Moon and Grandfather Sun were very happy with the four hundred boys – that is, with the stars flickering their tiny lights like pinpricks in the night. But soon enough the novelty of their creation seemed to pass.

"So what are we going to do with these stars, these four hundred flickering boys, who are as silent as the black sky in which they hang? Stars, speak to us!" Grandmother Moon and Grandfather Sun shouted together.

But the stars said nothing.

The grandparents were disappointed. "So now what are we going to do?" they asked each other.

Grandfather Sun once again noticed that sadness covered Grandmother Moon's face like a blue scar. And since his light was reflected in her face, he felt her sadness in his own heart. He was so angry that he made a sunspot explode. *Pow!* went the huge sunspot, lighting up several universes.

Grandfather Sun began pacing back and forth in the sky, which wasn't empty as it had been before. He bumped into the stars, and they shattered into little bits called meteorites. *Powww!* Thousands of star bits scattered and began to orbit the universe.

Sometimes at night we see a falling star with a long tail. It's because Grandfather Sun is walking along bumping into the stars at his feet. "What am I going to do to make my lovely Moon happy?" he'd ask. And *Powww!* Thousands of meteorites would shoot through the sky.

This made Grandmother Moon laugh hard. But the first meteorites Grandfather Sun created hit her, leaving marks on her pretty face. She didn't like this at all. So she learned to duck so that the meteorites sailed over her and she thought, "What can we create next so that we don't get bored?"

Both of them came up with the same idea at the same time.

"We'll create two great spirits who will be responsible for giving us happiness. We'll create the Heart of Earth and give her the Maya name Uk'u'x Ulew, and we'll create the Heart of Heaven and give him the Maya name Uk'u'x Kaj. The Heart of Earth will be the tender and affectionate mother of the creatures born from the power in her belly. And the Heart of Heaven will be the tender and affectionate father of the creatures born from the power in his belly. So it will be," said Grandmother Moon and Grandfather Sun.

They were so happy that they began to dance, forming a huge circle with the stars, which were really the four hundred boys. This is why the dancers wear masks representing the sun, the moon and the stars for the village festival. They dance all day long in memory of that time, so long ago, when Grandmother Moon and Grandfather Sun created our mother, the Heart of Earth, and our father, the Heart of Heaven.

The Creation of Plants, Animals and Fish

WHEN GRANDMOTHER MOON and Grandfather Sun grew tired of dancing, they called Mother Earth and Father Sky over to them.

"We are very bored living alone in the universe. We made the stars, but they don't speak. Now we want you to make creatures of all sizes and colors to bring joy to our hearts, so that there will be sounds in the universe, so that this huge black silence will become a symphony of colors, and everyone will live happily."

"Of course, Grandmother Moon, Grandfather Sun," said Mother Earth.

"So it shall be, Grandmother Moon, Grandfather Sun," said Father Sky.

And as if they were children given clay to make figurines, they happily began to make all sorts of things. First, they created the sea, and the earth was covered with the blue waters of one huge ocean.

"And now that we've created the sea," they said, "what shall we fill it with?"

"Fish!" they both said at once. And they amused themselves making fish, both large and small. The sea was like a huge party with all its creatures always on vacation!

The water of the sea was salty, and soon Mother Earth and Father Sky were thirsty. "Where will we find fresh water to drink?" they asked. There were no lakes, no rivers, no fountains – just a huge wide ocean!

So they spoke with their grandparents, who smiled and said, "To find fresh water, there must be land, and on this land springs, rivers and lakes."

Mother Earth and Father Sky were very happy and, like children, they began to make meadows, mountains, volcanoes, hills, canyons, ravines and jungles out of clay. And trees, so many trees that they didn't all fit on the land. And plants and herbs and flowers. The world was one huge green thicket. Even today's deserts were full of vegetation back then. Here and there they created rivers of fresh water, where their faces could be reflected, and where the stones were as polished and shiny as brand new jewels. And Mother Earth stretched across all the land she had created and merged with it. That's why Mother Earth is everywhere – she is the ground we walk on and the mountains we see.

For several centuries our grandparents were happy with what they saw, though they suspected that something was still missing. And it was true that something was missing, for while the ocean was a festival of flying fish, on the earth, plants and trees and flowers grew silently.

"The animals of the earth are missing!" Mother Earth and Father Sky cried together.

More pleased than ever, they began to shape animals out of clay. And all of a sudden the earth was filled with endless chatter, especially when they made birds, the noisiest creatures in

the whole universe. The birds flew from branch to branch singing, shouting and at times, even talking. Some, like the cackling macaws, created a loud, crazy quilt of noise and color. No one could sleep with the fuss the animals made! Mother Earth was happy with all the little creatures, like painted clay dolls, in her bosom.

Then Grandmother Moon and Grandfather Sun called Mother Earth and Father Sky over. "What you've created is beautiful. We're so happy to see water, in the sea and on the earth, to see fish in the sea and animals on land – those things that should be in one place and those in another. The noise from the sea and the earth is music to our ears. Surely we are not alone now."

A great happiness filled the hearts of Mother Earth and Father Sky when they heard their grandparents' words. But it came to an end when their grandparents said, "Something's still missing. We need a creature who can love and cry and is made of the stuff of nature. A creature who will have sons and daughters, grandsons and granddaughters and great-grandchildren, generation after generation, and who will live in goodness. A creature who will cross the breadth of time like a humble walker, like a simple traveler, like a gentle wanderer. A creature capable of thanking us."

So Mother Earth and Father Sky got down on their knees and asked their grandparents for the strength, the knowledge and the wisdom to create the fullness of life. The grandparents danced and danced amid lightning and endless thunder. It rained day and night, and life grew on the earth for all eternity.

The Keepers of the Earth

MOTHER EARTH called toward the Four Corners of the Universe, "Daughters of the earth, sons of the sun, sons of the sky, daughters of the clouds and the waters!"

Her cry echoed, "Earth…sun…sky…clouds…waters!"

Father Sky called toward the Four Corners of the Universe, "Everyone's invited to the party. Everyone join in!"

His words resounded, "Parrrty…Everyyyyone!"

His call reached all the creatures of creation. Their heads turned toward his powerful voice and they came by air, land and water – flying, slithering, walking and swimming – toward Mother Earth and Father Sky. And they came together, and stared at one another.

The elephant was perplexed to see a mouse so small, and the mouse to see an elephant so huge. The fly greeted his cousin the mosquito. The turtle raced with the hare. The alligator opened her huge snout, and a hummingbird approached to see what was inside. The armadillo showed off his warrior-like shell. The tiger greeted the cat and asked if, perhaps, they were related.

The bee was drunk on the sweetness of so many flowers. The owl nodded sleepily in the light, and the sloth, hanging from a branch, understood him perfectly well. The songbirds conversed with the parakeets, while the parrots gave lengthy speeches as if they were politicians.

How wonderful it was for all the creatures to learn about each other! And they talked and questioned, wanting to know each and every detail. The creatures laughed in their animal languages. Sometimes they didn't understand each other, but they all understood that they were the grandchildren of Grandmother Moon and Grandfather Sun and the children of Mother Earth, the Heart of Earth, and Father Sky, the Heart of Heaven. With their mysterious tongues they said, "Ajaw is our Creator."

And then Mother Earth and Father Sky began to take attendance.

"Jaguar!" they shouted.

"Present!" answered Jaguar.

And while they took attendance, Mother Earth and Father Sky told the creatures, "Now we will give you a chore for each and every day of your life. You must be the keepers of human beings, the *nahuales* of humankind."

"White-tailed deer!"

"Present."

"Brown deer!"

"Present."

"Gray deer, tigers, lions, wildcats, pumas…!"

"Present…present…present…present…"

"You will be the *nahuales*, the keepers who will sustain the power of the universe with your four paws."

"Coyotes, wolves, wild dogs…!"

"Present."

"You will be the *nahuales*, the keepers of justice. You will be the judges and the defenders of the truth. You will be the carriers of the signs and omens of the future."

"Owls of all types!"

"Present."

"You will be the *nahuales*, the keepers of death and the other world. You will be the messengers between the spirits of our ancestors and the spirits of the living."

"White bears and gray bears!"

"Present."

"You will be the *nahuales* of the snow, the fog, the rain and the rivers. You will be the permanent guardians of the air, and your breath will reach the Four Corners of the Universe."

And so it went for twenty days. Ajaw – the Heart of Earth, Mother Earth, the Heart of Heaven, Father Sky – went on calling the animals one by one, giving each its mission on the earth. And that's why each creature is a *nahual*, the keeper of something, because this is what Mother Earth and Father Sky decided.

Why the Elders Are the Four Corners of the Universe

Now I'm going to tell you what Ajaw – the Heart of Earth, Mother Earth, the Heart of Heaven, Father Sky – did after giving each animal his mission. He called all the elders of the world together.

"Chuchu'ib'!" he called the female elders.

"Tata'ib'!" he called the male elders.

Chuchu'ib' and Tata'ib' are the names given to the grandmothers and grandfathers. The elders began arriving from the Four Corners of the Universe, leaning on their pinewood canes with their withered wrinkled faces, their brown freckles and white hair, but with the nobility of ancient people.

"Chuchu'ib'!" he called the female elders.

"Tata'ib'!" he called the male elders.

Grandmothers and grandfathers dragged themselves to him with their toothless mouths, with their eyes that seemed not to see but saw all that is deep in our hearts. They had been walking the four paths of the earth for a long time – the red path, the white path, the yellow path and the black path – the four magical paths of wisdom. That's why they couldn't see things far off, but only those close up, with great depth.

"Chuchu'ib'!" called Ajaw, the Heart of Earth.

"Tata'ib'!" called Ajaw, the Heart of Heaven.

"Here we are," said the elders from beneath the hats that protected them from the sun. "We are also here to receive our mission."

Then Ajaw spoke to them. "Chuchu'ib', Tata'ib'! You, the elders of great birth, of great reverence, will be the paths and guides to direct the future of creation. You will be the columns, the guardians of the spirit of the Creator of the universe."

This is why our elders deserve respect from all women and men, girls and boys – they are the paths, the guides, the columns of the spirit of the universe. They are the advice and the experience. Within them is the treasure of lives that have seen the passage of time in their heads and hearts. This is why you must always let them pass before you. You must give them the places of honor, and you must always bow your head in respect. We owe so much to our grandmothers and grandfathers.

"Chuchu'ib', Tata'ib'! You are going to build cities all over the world. Each city will have its own songs, paintings, palaces and houses, temples and dances, prayers and pleasures, languages and books, poetry and music. And in each city the natural world will be reflected in all of these things. Chuchu'ib', Tata'ib'! Let each city be pleased with its own songs and dances, and let each also be happy with the songs and dances of others. The happiness of the world will sprout from these differences.

"Chuchu'ib', Tata'ib'! Our elder women and men! You will be given the power to talk to the wind, to the hills, to the roads. You will gain wisdom from talking to them, and you will pass it on to your daughters, sons, granddaughters, grandsons, so

that they will learn from nature how to live in peace with one another. They will know that the earth does not belong to them, but that they are part of it. The earth will be a sacred place, a place created for the dreams of all generations. Chuchu'ib', Tata'ib'! Thanks to your counsel, people will plant their dreams on the earth, and their dreams will blossom as if they were magic flowers."

The elders were in awe as they listened to Ajaw speak. They took off their straw hats to show that they accepted the mission they had been given. They made a pact with the Creator. And this is how the natural laws of creation were established.

To celebrate the occasion, Ajaw called lightning and thunder so that they could announce the great pact. The earth lit up with the white light of lightning and, a split second later, the sky shook with the drum roll of thunder. *Boooooom!* echoed back and forth between the clouds. *Boom! Boom! Boom! Boom!* This was the sign that the pact between Ajaw and the elders had been made.

Where It's Revealed That Each Thing Has a Spirit

EVERYTHING in the universe has a spirit. How many things are in the universe?

Lots.

Lots and lots and lots.

There are mountains and volcanoes, hills and ranges, rivers, streams, creeks and springs. There are plants and trees, stones and beaches and every single drop of ocean water. There are so many things in the universe!

You must know that each thing has a spirit. Best of all, this spirit has a name. The name we Maya give it is Rajaw Juyub'.

Rajaw Juyub', the spirit of everything in the universe.

Rajaw Juyub' slithers between the forest leaves like a snake, but isn't a snake. Rajaw Juyub' parts the waters like a fish, but isn't a fish. Rajaw Juyub' flies through the air like a bird, but isn't a bird.

Rajaw Juyub' is the keeper of everything in the universe. He sees everything in all the corners of nature. He is the four eyes floating in the mist, in the crystal air, in the reflection of water.

He sometimes appears, but he has no shape. A far-off whistle? It's Rajaw Juyub'. He is like a crackle, something passing that is seen and not seen.

When someone violates nature's laws, when someone cuts down trees, stealing away the oxygen, or removes the vegetation around lakes so that they dry up, when someone cuts down the mountain brush so that the mountains crumble, then Rajaw Juyub', the keeper of things, appears.

Whoever sees him is enchanted, as if sleeping with open eyes. They are like sleepwalkers. And later, when they awake from their long sleep, they remember speaking to someone, but don't remember him or what they talked about. They return to their homes saying, "I dreamed that I spoke to someone, but I don't remember with whom or about what." Then they fall ill and die.

But if they apologize, if they ask for forgiveness and make an offering to the Creator, then they will live a long time. Their hair will turn white and they will become respected elders.

Sometimes Rajaw Juyub' appears as a dog or a coyote or another kind of animal. Sometimes in the mountains we come across a creature roaming peacefully. It might be Rajaw Juyub', the one who judges the way people treat nature.

This is why the grandmothers and grandfathers of the Maya lands bring him candles and flowers, a lot of honey and other offerings.

Why You Can See a Rainbow When Deer Are Born

ONCE THERE WAS a very wicked man who refused to follow the teachings of our grandmothers and grandfathers,
those of Chuchu'ib' and Tata'ib'. He wanted only money and
riches. He didn't care if he destroyed trees, polluted rivers and
killed animals in his pursuit of wealth.

One day this man was walking up a mountain path when he
heard a bird singing.

"*Piich,*" went the bird.

The man kept on walking. What did he care if a bird sang?
He was only interested in money and riches.

Once again he heard the bird singing, "*Piich, piich, piich!*"
(It wasn't really a bird, but Rajaw Juyub', who had taken the
form of a bird's song.)

The man continued walking up the mountain, with no
other plan but to cut down trees and destroy the forest.
Suddenly, he came to a path he had never seen before. "How
strange," he thought. "I know every square inch of this mountain, and I've never seen this path."

Out of curiosity, he decided to follow it. But after half an hour, he was back at the spot where he had started. As if under a magic spell, he hadn't advanced at all.

Suddenly, a big black dog appeared, its tail as long as a horse's. The man was frightened and started walking again, this time more rapidly. But after an hour he found himself back at the point where he had started. Once again, there was the black dog with the long tail, growling menacingly.

"What's going on?" the man thought. "I've been walking for over an hour and I'm back where I started, facing this terrifying dog."

Just then he saw a village he had never seen before. It was full of big, comfortable-looking houses. "At least I've made it to a nice village," the man thought.

He came across a boy and a girl in the courtyard of their home. "Look!" the boy was whining. "Look what they've done to me." And he showed his sister his legs, which were full of cuts, as if he had been stabbed by a knife blade or machete. Blood flowed from his wounds.

The man was terrified. "What happened, child? Who hurt you like this?" he said.

The boy raised his eyes. "You did," he replied. "You stabbed me. You burned and killed my brothers."

Trembling, the man tried to defend himself. "I've done nothing to hurt you," he argued.

Just then the boy changed into a gorgeous jaguar with wounds all over his body, and the girl turned into a stalk of bleeding sugarcane. And they said to him, "This is the damage you cause when you cut down trees, chase after animals and pollute rivers."

The man realized that Rajaw Juyub' was speaking to him through the girl, the sugarcane, the boy and the jaguar. And he

realized that the bird whistle was also Rajaw Juyub'. He realized that he had damaged nature. He fell to his knees and asked for forgiveness. He asked for another chance to prove he wasn't wicked. He knelt for thirteen days until his knees were swollen.

Ajaw, the Heart of Earth and the Heart of Heaven, heard his prayers. "I can see you have repented," Ajaw said. "I will turn you into a man-animal. You will be human and deer at the same time. Your life will be devoted to showing humans and creatures how to live in peace with Mother Nature.

"A person can absorb wisdom like a sponge absorbs water. You will use your wisdom to teach other human beings. You will be a teacher, a deer-teacher."

So the man became a wise man and walked the paths of the earth, sharing his wisdom. He walked everywhere – sometimes as a man, sometimes as a deer – until his hair turned as white as ocean foam. The day he died, the sun shone brightly and the sky was blue. Then it started to drizzle and a rainbow appeared. Since then, whenever there's a rainbow, people say that a baby deer is being born.

Where It's Told That Monkeys Are Descended from Humans

LONG AGO there were four brothers who loved each other very much. Ch'owen and Jun B'atz' were farmers. Jun aj Pu and Ix B'alam Kej were hunters.

Ch'owen and Jun B'atz' woke up every day before the sun rose. They drank a pot of coffee and ate a few tortillas with beans. Then when the sun was barely a reddish line etched against the mountains, they went into the fields. From morning till noon they scattered seeds or tended the plants once the seeds had sprouted. In the afternoon, after eating tortillas with avocado and drinking the jug of fresh corn gruel that their grandmother brought them, they worked the earth until sundown. They were wonderful workers.

Jun aj Pu and Ix B'alam Kej had another kind of life. Since they were hunters, they sometimes got up very early, like their brothers. But at other times they slept until the sun had taken many steps across the sky. They would go into the fields and sit down, waiting to shoot animals with their blowguns. If a pheasant suddenly appeared, *Wham!* A little stone would kill him. If a rabbit appeared, *Whop!* He'd be shot at once. And if the brothers saw a fat bird in the trees, *Ping!* She would fall to the ground, shot dead by one of them.

One day Ch'owen and Jun B'atz' got angry. "Our brothers spend the whole day singing and telling stories," they said. "They just sit around shooting their blowguns. Then they go to bed."

They were so angry that they decided to teach their brothers a lesson. They grabbed Jun aj Pu and Ix B'alam Kej by their throats and forced them to walk over a field of thorns. But the brothers felt no pain. On the contrary, they became drowsy, yawned happily and fell asleep on the field of thorns.

This enraged Ch'owen and Jun B'atz'. "How is it that when we throw them on thorns they fall asleep instead of weeping? We have to find a better punishment!"

So they grabbed Jun aj Pu and Ix B'alam Kej by their throats and took them to a field where ants flowed from a huge anthill like a rushing black river. They threw their brothers on the anthill. "Now the ants will sting them and they'll run off kicking and screaming," they thought. Instead, the hunters yawned pleasantly and fell asleep.

Then one day Jun aj Pu and Ix B'alam Kej came back from hunting in the mountains empty-handed. Their grandmother was furious. "Why haven't you brought anything back today?" she complained.

"Grandmother, we shot many birds, but they got tangled up in the tree vines. We need help to get them down."

Their grandmother ordered them to go back and gather the birds they had shot. She sent Ch'owen and Jun B'atz' to help them.

When Ch'owen and Jun B'atz' reached the trees, Jun aj Pu and Ix B'alam Kej said, "Could you go up and bring down the birds? We can't climb that high."

33

Ch'owen and Jun B'atz' immediately climbed the tree. But when they were nearly at the top, the tree began to shake. The branches started to pull away from them and the trunk thickened, forming a giant tree with huge leaves. The brothers got stuck way, way up at the top. They were like two tiny dots when seen from below.

"Help!" they cried. "We can't climb down! The tree's too tall!"

Jun aj Pu and Ix B'alam Kej shouted, "Loosen your sashes and tie one end to a branch. We'll come up and help you!"

So Ch'owen and Jun B'atz' took off their sashes and each tied one end to a branch. As if by magic, the sashes became tails and hair began growing on the brothers' faces, arms, chests, backs and legs. Their mouths stretched out and their noses flattened. They couldn't speak. The only sound that came out of their mouths was a very loud howl, like a lion's roar. They had become monkeys.

Hearing the lion's roar, their grandmother rushed to the mountains to see what was happening. When she saw that her grandchildren had been turned into monkeys that scratched their heads, stuck out their tongues, curled their tails, ate bananas and roared as loud as ten lions, she fell to the ground, laughing.

"From now on, you will be known as howler monkeys," she said to them. "You will live in the trees forever. You will be the keepers of the seasons, announcing the coming of storms and downpours so that men and women will be able to reach home without getting wet. You will represent the monkeys in their dealings with humans."

Ch'owen and Jun B'atz' happily accepted their fate as monkeys on one condition. "When it's time for the village festival, we want to turn back into boys so that we can play and dance like everyone else."

"So it shall be," their grandmother answered.

And when the next village festival came, they climbed down from the trees and became the boys they had once been, even though much time had passed! The first thing they did was to look for their brothers. They embraced one another and told jokes and laughed together. Then they went to their grandmother's house and played till they were exhausted.

Since Ch'owen and Jun B'atz' lived in the mountains, they had learned the secrets of the water, the earth, the wind and the sun. They also knew the secrets of the trees and footpaths, the mysteries of the streams, the confessions of the hills. They had so much to tell it would take more than a lifetime to do so. When the villagers found out that the friendly howler monkeys were among them, they asked for the secrets of the new world they lived in.

Using their magic powers, the monkey brothers transported the tallest tree in the jungle to the center of the village. They stripped off all the leaves from the branches and climbed as high as they could. Then they fastened their tails to the top and swung in the air, making faces, scratching their bellies and jumping from branch to branch to make the villagers laugh. The women went "*he, he, he,*" and the men went "*ha, ha, ha.*" And from that moment on, this monkey dance came to be known as the "Palo Volador" or the "Flying Pole."

When the festival ended, the monkey brothers' hearts filled with sadness because they had to return to the jungle. They tried to steal away so that no one would be sad to see them go. But Jun aj Pu and Ix B'alam Kej saw them and ran after them, and the other villagers ran after the brothers.

So the monkeys said to one another, "We've got to scare them so that they'll go back.

"If you don't go back to the village, we'll whip you with our tails," they said, running toward the villagers with their tails in their hands. And it turned into a game, especially for the girls and boys. The monkeys ran toward them and they would scamper off, dying of laughter. They played this game all day, till the villagers were so tired that they stretched out like drunks and fell asleep on the ground. And then the monkey brothers went back into the jungle without the villagers knowing.

This is why a few people always dress up as monkeys and chase the villagers, especially the girls and boys, when the Maya celebrate their village festival. Everyone knows that they are the howler monkey brothers saying goodbye.

The Story of the Weasel Who Helped People Find Corn

BEFORE THE MAYA discovered corn, they used to eat the roots of a delicious plant called Uk'u'x wa. Then the rains stopped. At first no one cared because there were huge bushes of Uk'u'x wa.

But with the drought, the bushes soon disappeared. The grandmothers and grandfathers went deep into the forests searching for the plant and would end up lost in the mountains.

"No more roots for us to eat!" they said sadly, when they returned.

Hunger bore into their stomachs like fistfuls of spines.

"The food's all gone!" the grandmothers said.

"What are we going to do?" asked the grandfathers.

Sorrow settled over the spirit of the people. The children started crying and begging for food.

"We have nothing," their parents told them.

The parents wept because they could not feed their children, and the grandmothers and grandfathers wept because it made them very sad to see their children and grandchildren crying.

One day a weasel came by and saw the people crying. "What's wrong?" she said. "Why do you have such long weepy faces when you should be dancing and celebrating?"

"Oh, Miss Weasel, if you only knew," a grandmother said.

"Oh, if you only knew, Miss Weasel," a grandfather said.

The weasel stared at them, confused, and went over to a tearful young couple. "I ran into a grandmother and a grandfather who were weeping," she said to them. "And you two are also crying. What's wrong?"

"Oh, Miss Weasel, if you only knew," the woman said.

"Oh, if you only knew, Miss Weasel," the man said.

More confused than ever, the weasel ran into two children. "Kids, I met your grandmother and grandfather, your mother and father, and they're all crying. And now I bump into you, and you're crying, too. Can you tell me what's wrong?"

"We're hungry and there's no more food," they wept.

The weasel was so upset she almost began to cry herself. She decided to help them. She brought together all the grandmothers, mothers, grandfathers, fathers, girls and boys. "I know a place where there's food," she said, her smile revealing her teeth and gums.

"Where, where, where?" the people asked anxiously.

"On a hill called Chwajuyub'. But you can't go there empty-handed. You have to make a pilgrimage, playing instruments and banging drums. You have to bring lots of flowers and perform all kinds of rituals and burn *ocote*..."

"We'll do it," the grandmothers and grandfathers promised.

"And when you're finished, you'll find a *pek* rock," the weasel said dramatically, holding her breath. "Under that rock, you'll find something known as corn, which grows all over..."

The people could hardly believe the weasel. It all sounded so wonderful. "It can't be true," they argued. "You're lying to us."

"I give you my word of honor as a weasel," she said. "You will find corn under the *pek* rock."

The people still had their doubts. So the weasel said, "Fine, I'll go with you and show you where the corn is hidden."

The villagers organized a huge procession and they carried all kinds of flowers – red geraniums, fire-colored bougainvillea, delicate orchids, bright carnations, perfumed roses. There were so many flowers that the people couldn't even be seen beneath them. They were like columns of army ants carrying food. And they carried their *ocote* torches and banged on their drums. The sharp notes from their flutes floated in the midst of the sweet-smelling flowers. It was amazing to see the villagers marching behind the weasel.

They walked and walked and walked until they reached a forest clearing. There they performed rites, burned *pom* and played sacred music. "This is the spot," the weasel told them. "Now, perfume the air with your flowers, light up your *ocote* torches and let the flutes and drums play together." The villagers did as they were told and then waited. They waited and waited.

Suddenly, they heard howler monkey cries announcing the coming of rain. First came big drops, like coins of water flung down from the sky. They splashed on the ground, raising dust. And then the drops thickened till the gusts of wind formed curtains of rain. *Rrrrrrrrrrrm!* The curtains opened and shut. The rain fell from the sky as if huge jugs of water were being poured. The children ran, jumping from puddle to puddle, splashing one another and laughing.

A flash of lightning suddenly whitened the trees, the leaves and the faces of the villagers. The children shot off to their parents for protection. *Boooom!* A huge roll of thunder echoed on the horizon.

Finally, a bolt of lightning struck the *pek* rock. The rock split open, releasing a wisp of gray smoke. *Booooom!* rumbled the thunder from behind the mountains.

When it stopped raining, the villagers ran to see what was under the rock. There were tons and tons of corn kernels, enough food for everyone! The corn struck by lightning was all black. The corn farthest away from it was white, and the corn in the middle was either red or yellow.

Then the villagers said, "We need to take the corn back to our houses. But first we need to separate the different kernels so that we can plant them and harvest them year after year."

This is how the Maya were introduced to the four varieties of corn.

They planted black kernels and black corn shot up. The yellow kernels gave them yellow corn, the red kernels, red, and the white, white. The husks, however, were all alike – green leaves curling at the edges. And from then on, corn was the food of the people.

When the villagers had had enough to eat, they decided to honor the weasel.

"Miss Weasel," they said, "you knew what you were talking about. We want to throw you a huge party."

The weasel blinked several times as if to say, "You didn't believe me?"

The villagers agreed to give her the best hens, roosters and turkeys they had. Some brought her hens they had fattened with corn. Others brought roosters that had grown plump from pecking the new food, and still others brought their red-throated turkeys as an offering.

But since there are always cheats, some villagers hid their best hens and roosters and brought the weasel the smallest of chicks. The weasel noticed how miserly these villagers were and decided to teach them a lesson, for you must always give thanks for a gift.

That evening, as everyone slept, the weasel went back to the village. She snuck into the hen houses of the misers and stole all their fat hens, roosters and turkeys.

This is how the weasel taught us not to be miserly and to be grateful for what we are given.

The Man Who Became a Buzzard

THERE ONCE was a very lazy man. Everything was a chore to him. Waking up in the morning was hard, but when he went to work in the fields, his pickax seemed as heavy as the world upon his shoulders. He would sit on a rock and yawn. Finally, he would get up, cursing his fate for having been born a man to work the earth.

This man would look at the birds and sigh and shake his head. He was sad not to be one of them. He was most jealous of the buzzard that flew up high, floating in the air, turning in circles – pure suspension of weightless feathers in the vault of the sky.

"Gosh, if I were a buzzard," he said, "I'd float in the air, letting gusts carry me while I slept, and I'd eat free food all day!"

He had barely said this when a buzzard appeared at his side.

"I heard what you just said," the buzzard exclaimed, stirring his black wings. "And I'm bored being a buzzard. Why don't we trade places? I'll become a man and you a buzzard. If at the end of three days we're not happy, we can go back to being what we were."

The man was thrilled. "I accept your proposal," he said. "But there's just one problem."

"What is it?"

"I don't know what a buzzard does and you don't know what a man does. We have to explain to each other what we do."

"You're right," the buzzard answered. "So tell me what you do."

"Well," the man began. "Every day I go out into the fields with my tools. I have to work hard so the corn will grow and we have a good harvest. When I return home, I clean my tools, wash my hands and eat dinner with my wife. If I'm sweaty, I take a steam bath to remove all the dirt."

"Sounds fine to me," the buzzard answered. "I, on the other hand, fly through the air all day looking for something to eat. Whenever I see a little wisp of smoke, I know I will find food. I swoop down and grab my meal, which usually consists of dead animals. When I can't find anything else, I eat poop."

The man thought he was more clever. Instead of eating carrion and dung, he would find a hearty meal for himself when he became a buzzard.

So they changed places. The man turned into a buzzard and the buzzard into a man. They said goodbye, planning to meet in three days to see how the experiment had worked.

The buzzard stayed in the fields and began to work the soil. After an hour he was sweating and panting. The tools slipped from his hands and nothing turned out right. All he wanted to do was lie down for a bit and regain his strength. "Honestly, it's hard being a man!" he said. But since he wanted to see what it was like, he did all the chores. In the afternoon, as the sun was about to set, he went home, dead-tired.

"I'm home," he told his wife, and began to clean his tools and put them away.

The woman looked at him, thinking, "How strange my husband seems today! He really stinks of sweat!"

Actually, he didn't stink of sweat but of buzzard, because buzzards are known the world over for their foul odor.

"My love, my darling, you need to take a bath," his wife told him.

The steam bath was in a very tiny room, filled with huge hot rocks. When you threw water over the rocks, the room filled with steam and you began to sweat. After sweating for a while, you threw a few cups of water over yourself and washed up.

His wife brought the buzzard to the bath, telling him that she couldn't bear the stench. The buzzard had never seen a steam bath in his life. His wife threw lots and lots of cold water on the burning stones and locked him in. Soon steam was everywhere and the poor buzzard began to sweat. He was afraid he would never be able to fly again, his feathers felt so heavy. He thought he was going to suffocate with his feathers glued to his skin.

His wife finally opened the door. Realizing that he still stank, she threw more water over the burning stones. Once again, a cloud of steam enveloped the buzzard. He began to cough and choke. Everything was dark. He continued to sweat, his feathers dripping. His wife kept throwing more water on the stones because she couldn't rid him of the stench. How could she? He was a buzzard, after all.

Finally, when the stones were cool, his wife poured a huge jug of cold water over him. The buzzard gasped for breath. He opened his mouth but couldn't talk – a shudder as light as a feather raced up and down his body. He thought he would die.

"So this is what a man's life is all about!" he thought. "I'd rather be a buzzard!"

Meanwhile, the man flew happily up into the sky. He sang as gusts of wind carried him from here to there. "This is the life," he said. "No more work in the cornfields. Whenever I'm hungry, I'll look for a little wisp of smoke, swoop down and eat for free!" He circled in the air, greeting all his buzzard friends, who were astonished to see him so happy.

Soon he felt pangs of hunger. In the distance he saw a little wisp of smoke. "Now let's see how this works," he said to himself. He began to turn in circles and then flung himself down like an arrow.

What a mistake! Some men were burning dry brush in preparation for the harvest, and the poor buzzard-man ended up scorching his feathers. "Oh, no!" he screamed, flapping his wings in the flames. The men laughed and laughed to see such a foolish buzzard.

Somehow he was able to get back into the air, but his wings stung and he was even hungrier. He was so hungry that he didn't think twice when he saw another wisp of smoke ahead of him. Again, he swept down with all his might and found a huge mound of poop. He barely managed to avoid crashing into it. "I certainly can't eat this!" he thought. And once more he rose back up into the sky.

And this is how he passed the day. He was fooled each time he saw a wisp of smoke. When it wasn't a fire, it was poop. And when it wasn't poop, it was rotten meat. He hadn't eaten a thing and he was dying of hunger.

Three days passed, and the man and the buzzard met at the agreed-upon location. The buzzard had lost half his feathers, and the few that remained looked as if they had been scared to death. He had calluses everywhere from all the work. His eyes bulged because his wife complained so much about his foul smell that he couldn't sleep.

The man was extremely thin, barely a wisp of air. He had a long beard and his eyes spun about from hunger.

"How did it go for you, Mr. Buzzard?" the man asked.

"Terribly!" the buzzard answered. "The work's hard, the harvest poor. I sweat too much and the bath ruins my feathers. I want to go back to my buzzard life. How did it go for you?"

"Horribly!" the man responded. "Too much flying, too much circling, all this freedom and nothing to eat – unless I want to eat poop all day. I want to go back to my human life!"

And so with great relief, they both went back to being what they were.

Our grandmothers and grandfathers say that this story teaches us that men and women are workers. Work gives people dignity, while laziness means you eat what the buzzard eats.

Twins Make Holes in Your Clothes and Send Ants

YOU MUST KNOW that twins are very special. We Mayas call them *laj tyox*, which means "small altar." When we see twins passing in the street, we give them little gifts – a few pennies, a special present, a few kind words.

When they're young, twins speak a special language to one another and their parents can't understand a word. Their parents give them equal shares of everything so that the twins won't become angry – the same food, the same clothes. Their trips and games are exactly the same.

Because if twins get angry, boy, can they be vengeful! For example, if you're eating a juicy mango or a ripe banana and don't offer them a bite, they're liable to send ants to plague you. And you shouldn't eat grilled corn unless you share a few kernels with them.

If they get very angry, they can make holes in your clothes. Suddenly, you notice that your shirt is full of holes and think that maybe it was attacked by moths. Or you realize that your best sweater has a hole in the front, and you think a termite

made it. No way! You've probably insulted a twin and so he has made holes in your clothes.

Once there was a set of twins who lived happily with their grandparents and parents. One day the parents started to argue – this is mine and that's yours. They had a huge argument. The grandmother got so angry when she saw her children fighting that she decided that she and the grandfather would take their grandchildren away. And since the grandparents always spoiled the twins, they were happy to go with them.

But one day the grandmother decided to go back and visit her daughter. She packed her things and left without saying her usual goodbye. The twins didn't like this at all, and they started crying and crying. Their crying was unbearable. Their grandfather gave them candy, but they went on crying. He brought them a basket of fruit, but they kept on crying. For three days they wept in the morning, in the afternoon and, worst of all, all through the night. Their grandfather was desperate.

Three days later the grandmother returned. "Why haven't the twins let me go on my trip in peace?" she asked. As soon as they saw her, the twins fell asleep with smiles on their faces.

"Why did you come back so soon?" the grandfather asked her.

"The twins sent me a message. They wanted me to come back," she explained.

"And what message did they send?"

"As soon as I reached our daughter's house, ants started to show up everywhere. We looked all over for the anthill, but couldn't find it. All we could see were orderly rows of ants, like soldiers, going through the door, running along the walls, circling around the house. The ants climbed up our legs and stung and tickled us! They were devilish ants! We put fistfuls of salt on all the paths and entrances, but the ants kept appearing from other places. We couldn't eat because there were ants on the table. We couldn't sit because there were ants on the chairs. We couldn't sleep because there were ants in the beds. I haven't slept a wink for three days! That's when I knew that the twins were sending me a message to come back."

The grandfather burst out laughing. Meanwhile, the twins slept soundly in their double bed.

That's how twins are. If you hurt one, the other comes to his defense. If you scold them unfairly, they both get upset and punish you in a mysterious way. They can even send scorpions instead of ants. If one twin picks up a disease from a cat, then the other twin lends his sick brother his life force – the cat had better watch out because a twin has ten lives while a cat only has nine. When two sets of twins come together, there's lots of whispering – *psssssst, pssst, psssssst, psssssst*. Who knows what they're planning in their secret language?

That's why twins are worthy of respect and admiration – they have special powers. They are the descendants of the twins who founded the world.

Now I will tell you a story about these famous twins from our sacred book, the Popol Vuh, which we call the Pop Wuj.

The Amazing Twins

I N A N C I E N T T I M E S, when there were no clocks and time passed without passing, Jun aj Pu and Ix B'alam Kej, the sacred twins, the founders of the universe, would play ball.

Thump! Thump! Thump! went the ball as it bounced off their knees and shoulders and the walls of the ballcourt. *Thump!* as they gave it a header.

Underground, the Lords of Evil heard the *Thump! Thump! Thump!* of the ball. Many, many years earlier they had defeated the twins' father in that same game. "Someone is playing above us on Mother Earth," they said. "It must be the twins, Jun aj Pu and Ix B'alam Kej. We'll challenge them to a game, just as we did their fathers."

And so they sent a louse with the message to come down at once to the kingdom of the Lords of the Underworld to play ball.

As if by magic, the louse fell onto the lap of the twins' grandmother. "Grandmother," the louse said. "I come from the Lords of the Underworld with a message for Jun aj Pu and Ix B'alam Kej. They must appear within a week to play ball against them."

The grandmother said, "But how can I tell them? Their court is very far away and I can barely walk!"

"Don't worry," the louse answered. "I'll tell them myself."

And the louse flew off toward the field where the twins were playing. But he was a tiny louse and he could only fly ten yards an hour. "I'll never get there in time," he thought.

Just then he bumped into a toad who said, "Where are you going, louse, so eagerly and so quickly?"

"I'm going to the ballcourt with a message for the twins. But at my speed, I'll never get there," he explained, all aflutter.

"Don't worry," the toad answered. "I'll give you a hand." And, *Gulp!* Out flashed his long tongue and he swallowed the louse.

The toad began to run – back then he had four very normal legs. Still, after an hour, he had only gone a hundred yards and the ballcourt was very far away. "I'll never get there in time," he thought.

Just then he bumped into a huge snake. In those days, toads and snakes were good friends, and they'd spend the afternoons chatting away.

"Where are you going in such a hurry?" the snake asked.

"I have a message for Jun aj Pu and Ix B'alam Kej," said the toad. "But no matter how fast I run, it's not fast enough."

"Don't worry," the snake answered. "I'll give you a hand. And, *Gulp!* He swallowed the toad.

The snake slithered away making a racket like the wind blowing through the leaves. He was crossing a field when an eagle flying in the sky spotted him.

"I wonder where the snake is going so quickly?" he asked himself. He shot down to the field like an arrow and landed in front of the snake. "What's wrong, snake? What's your hurry?"

"I have an urgent message for the twins, who are playing ball, but at this speed I won't get there in time," the snake lamented.

"Don't worry," the eagle told him. "I'll give you a hand." With that, he swallowed, *Gulp!* And the snake ended up in the eagle's belly. The eagle rose into the air and was soon flying over the field where the boys were playing.

But the twins, who were great hunters, saw the eagle and weren't going to let their chance escape. *Bock! Bock! Bock!* They shot him down with their blowguns.

"Oh, my eye!" the eagle cried. "I have a message for you," he said to the twins, "but if you don't heal my eye, I won't give it to you."

Curious to hear what he had to say, the twins magically healed the eagle's eye. "Now give us the message."

"I have it here in my belly," he said. And *burp*, he coughed up the snake.

The twins asked the snake, "What's the message you're bringing us?"

"I have it here in my belly," he said. And *burp*, the snake coughed up the toad.

The twins asked the toad, "What's the message?"

But the toad couldn't speak because the louse was stuck between his teeth. "*Burp, burp, burp,*" said the toad.

The twins got angry, because they thought he was making fun of them. And without thinking twice, they threw a rock at the toad and broke his legs. This is why toads hop along the ground.

But the blow forced the toad to spit out the louse who finally gave the twins the message: "The Lords of the Underworld are waiting for you in their kingdom under Mother Earth."

And so the twins went to play ball with the Lords of the Underworld. And from then on it was established that toads eat insects, snakes eat toads and eagles eat snakes. That's how things happened in that time without time.

The Story of the Hormigo Tree

T HE HORMIGO TREE woke up feeling sad. There was no
reason for this. It was a splendid morning. The other trees
woke up happily, with squirrels racing from one leaf-covered
branch to another. The birds broke into song just before the sun
rose as if all days were holidays. The hormigo tree had nothing
to be sad about and yet it woke up feeling sad.

The hormigo tree is a huge, sturdy tree with very green
leaves and hard wood, the hardest of all the trees in the jungle.
The woodpecker's strong beak, so expert at making holes in
trees, simply bounces off the trunk of this tree. Maybe it's
because there are no woodpeckers that the hormigo tree seems
to be a home for other birds.

All the jungle birds would fly to it – grackles, mockingbirds,
buglers, motmots, sparrows. They would alight on the branches of the hormigo tree and sing their ancient music, as old as the
world itself. And their music would enter the hormigo tree
through its leaves, branches and sap till it reached its very heart.
And the more the birds sang, the more the hormigo tree filled

up with music. And the moment came when the hormigo tree was so full of music that it felt it would burst.

The hormigo tree wanted to sing, but it couldn't. It had no mouth like humans, no beak like birds. It realized that the whole universe sang. The sea roared when it was angry, its breakers crashing against the shore. Ravines answered with an echo whenever anyone called them. Streams said incomprehensible things as their waters leaped from stone to stone. Caves in the hills ululated.

The hormigo tree noticed that all the animals sang as well. Jaguars and howler monkeys roared, coyotes and wolves howled, other monkeys screamed – every single animal sang as best he could. The hormigo tree realized that the Heart of Heaven and the Heart of Earth had created a musical world. And it was the only one, bursting with the desire to sing, that remained silent in the middle of the jungle!

This was why the hormigo tree woke up feeling sad.

"Isn't it enough that the wind whistles through your leaves?" a squirrel asked.

"That's not good enough," it answered. "I want the gift of music that animals, streams and rivers have."

The hormigo tree knew that it was the fate of trees to be silent, but it wanted to sing and release from its heart all the trills the birds had sung throughout its life. The hormigo tree sighed. It was suffering from nostalgia – the illness of a dream, a desire, a longing.

The worst thing is that nostalgia is contagious. Soon the birds living in the hormigo tree branches stopped singing. They, too, were sad and instead of singing they breathed deeply as if about to swoon. And the birds from nearby trees were upset to discover that each time they wanted to trill or screech, only a deep sigh came out. It was as if they had lost their hearts in a ravine's darkest corner and had no strength to look for them. And the disease spread to all the birds and from the birds to the other animals. Dogs stopped barking and looked about with their familiar sad gaze. Monkeys stopped crying and bent their heads, their stares lost on the horizon. Lions wouldn't even let out their tremendous yawns.

And from the animals the nostalgia illness spread to the streams, which stopped gurgling, and to the oceans, which remained calm, as if there were no wind. Even the wind stopped whistling. In time, the world now mute became deaf as well.

And then the Heart of Heaven and the Heart of Earth heard the huge silence that stretched across the universe. "What's happened?" they asked. "What's this silence all about?

They asked the hills and rivers who replied, "Surely the wind has an answer."

And they asked the wind who answered them humbly, "Father and Mother, sadness is the reason why all the animals of the land, sea and air are silent. It spread from one animal to another until it reached the Four Corners of the Universe. But the beginning of this tragedy is in the heart of the jungle – the sadness that attacked the hormigo tree."

So the Heart of Heaven and the Heart of Earth visited the hormigo tree and asked what was wrong.

"Mother and Father," the tree answered. "I'm sorry to have infected the whole universe with my gloom. Over the years I've been saturated with music, and I'm not satisfied with having only the whistling of the wind as it rustles my leaves. Mother and Father, I want to sing. I need to release all the powerful music that lives inside me!"

The Heart of Earth, Mother Nature, answered the hormigo tree, "Don't be so sad now. You should know that everything in life plays a role to ensure peace. You also know that each and

every thing has its own way of expressing what it feels to the rest of the world. The trees whistle with the help of the wind – in the same way the caves ululate and the rivers and streams sing."

She went on speaking, "And yet your sadness has affected us. We will consult Grandfather Sun and Grandmother Moon and, tomorrow at daybreak, a beautiful feathered quetzal will land on your highest branch and whisper the message of our grandparents in your ear.

"Don't be sad, son of ours. We want to see you happy again so that all the animals in the air, in the water and on the land will once more fill the Four Corners of the Universe with sound." Then the Heart of Heaven and the Heart of Earth left the hormigo tree.

The following day, at the first gleam of light, a quetzal with glowing green feathers appeared. He lit on the highest branch of the hormigo tree.

"Grandmother Moon has spoken," the quetzal began. "She sends you a shower of jade dust to wash away the sadness that has infected your roots, trunk, branches and leaves. From now on, you will only spread happiness and the desire to live from the very heart of the jungle. Your seed will spread through the jungles and thousands of hormigo trees will populate the earth."

The quetzal took a deep breath and then continued, "Grandmother Moon has decided that the fate of trees is to whistle in the wind and that singing is not part of your nature. And yet Grandmother has been so moved by your sadness that she will give you the gift of music. She entrusted me to explain what will happen in the future.

"The Men of Corn will be created to populate the earth and honor the memory of their fathers and grandfathers. The Men of Corn will possess wisdom and will learn to make the earth produce. They will also cultivate the arts and sciences. Women and men will have the gift of music in their souls, given to them by their Makers and Creators."

The quetzal continued, "The Men of Corn will discover that the wood of the hormigo tree contains the spirit of all bird-song. They will cut your wood into long and short slats and will call them keys. The keys will be tied together on top of huge dry gourds. And when these keys are struck by a wooden mallet with a rubber ball at the end, the purest of sounds, the most pleasant music in the universe, will be heard. It will fill the mountain air with the same peacefulness as the rain in the afternoons or with the softness of streams flowing from the mountains or with the squawking of birds in the early mornings. This instrument made by men will release the music in your heart and will be called the marimba. It will bring pleasure to the ears of the people during their festivals and dances, as well as during periods of rest and reflection. Only in this way will the music you treasure be released."

And this is how the hormigo tree came to be used to make the marimba. From the time the Men of Corn were created, their spirits released the gift of music that the Makers and Creators had given them. And they knew that deep inside the hormigo tree slept the music that would make their festivals happy and teach them to dance. This music would also accompany their sadness, so that they would remember the time that the hormigo tree was infected with gloom.

● ● ●

These are the stories Grandmother and Grandfather told me. I am telling them to you exactly as they told them to me. They are old stories, as old as the world is old, and they should be heard at night, sitting around a fire, just before you shut your eyes and begin to dream.

GLOSSARY

Ajaw: Maya god comprised of the Heart of Earth and the Heart of Heaven
Chuchu'ib': female elders
Huipil: colorful woven blouse worn by Maya women
Laj tyox: Maya for twins, literally "small altar"
Marimba: musical instrument with graduated wooden keys, which are struck
   with a mallet
Nahual: animal spirit, companion
Ocote: resinous pine wood used in torches
Palo Volador: kind of a dance, literally "flying pole"
Pek: rock under which the sacred corn is found
Pom: incense
Popul Vuh or Pop Wuj: sacred book of the Maya, one of the oldest books in
   the Americas
Quetzal: bird of Central America, sacred to the Maya, having brilliant green
   and red feathers; the national bird of Guatemala
Rajaw Juyub': spirit of the universe
Tata'ib': male elders
Uk'u'x Kaj: Heart of Heaven
Uk'u'x Ulew: Heart of Earth
Uk'u'x wa: bushy plant with edible roots